LAZY DAVE

JARVIS

HARPER
An Imprint of HarperCollinsPublishers

Lazy Dave

Copyright © 2015 by Peter Jarvis

All rights reserved. Manufactured in China.

www.harpercollinschildrens.com

ISBN 978-0-06-235598-0 (trade bdg.)

The artist used pencil, paint, and chalk to create the digital illustrations for this book.
Typography by Jeanne L. Hogle
15 16 17 18 19   SCP   10 9 8 7 6 5 4 3 2 1
❖
First Edition

FOR MY JENNA

Y A W N

This is Dave.

Like most dogs,
Dave loved to sleep.

He slept in
the bath.

He slept in
the laundry.

He even slept in Lilly's bed.

"You're the *laziest* dog in the world," said Lilly.
"Why are you so tired all the time? All you do
is sleep!"

But as soon as Lilly left for school each day . . .

Dave would get up
and go for a walk.

Because what Lilly didn't know
was that Dave was a *sleepwalker.*

He chased a confused cat up a tree.

He won first prize at
the Best Dog Show.

Dave sleepwalked where no dogs had ever been.

On Monday he kept his balance.

On Tuesday he was on top of the world.

On Wednesday he danced with an octopus.

On Thursday he faced his fears.

On Friday he was
off like a rocket.

One day, Dave was sleepwalking past the jewelry shop just as a thief was making a getaway!

The thief tripped over sleepwalking Dave, and the diamonds flew out of his grasp.

After that, Dave was a *hero.*
Even the mayor wanted to meet him!

Everybody wanted their
picture taken with Dave.

Dave got home just before
Lilly returned from school.

"Oh, Dave. You haven't moved *all* day!
Come on. It's time for a walk."

On their walk, Lilly heard about the dog who had stopped the *biggest* diamond crook in history.

"Too bad you can't be more like that dog," said Lilly.

"But don't worry, lazy Dave.
I love you just the way you are."

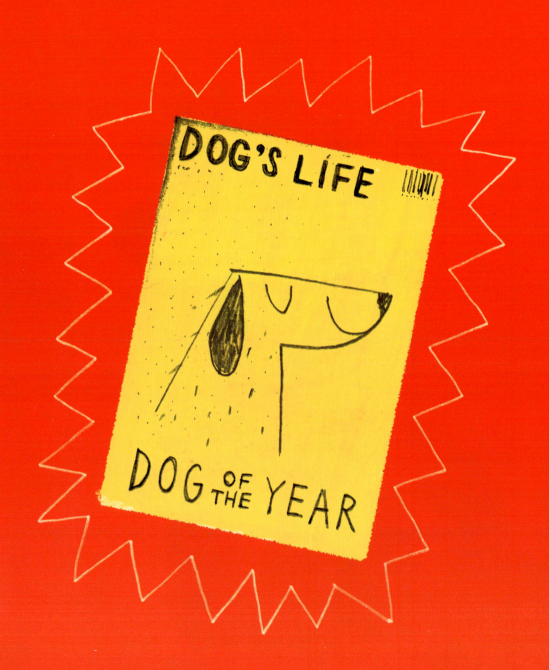